Drawing DOGS & CATS

A STEP-BY-STEP FUN GUIDE

Published by: **Watermill Press**
Mahwah, New Jersey

ISBN 0-8167-1667-6

Manufactured in the United States of America

BY DRAWING A SERIES OF SHORT LINES NEXT TO EACH OTHER – (AROUND THE BASIC SHAPES)

-OR SHORT ZIGZAG LINES-

(AROUND THE BASIC SHAPES)

-YOU WILL GET THE LOOK OF HAIR IN YOUR DRAWINGS OF DOGS OR CATS.

DRAW YOUR PICTURE HERE
DRAWING TIPS
IRISH SETTER
ALWAYS DRAW THE FIRST 2 STEPS LIGHTLY IN PENCIL UNTIL YOU ARE HAPPY WITH THE WAY YOUR DRAWING LOOKS.
1 JUST DRAW BASIC SHAPES
2 START TO ADD BASIC DETAILS
3
ERASE GUIDE LINES AND COMPLETE YOUR DRAWING.
DON'T BE AFRAID TO ERASE!
ADD DETAILS SUCH AS PAWS, HAIR, AND BLACK AREAS ONLY AFTER YOU'VE COMPLETED THE FIRST 2 BASIC STEPS.
HAVE FUN!

PUPPY

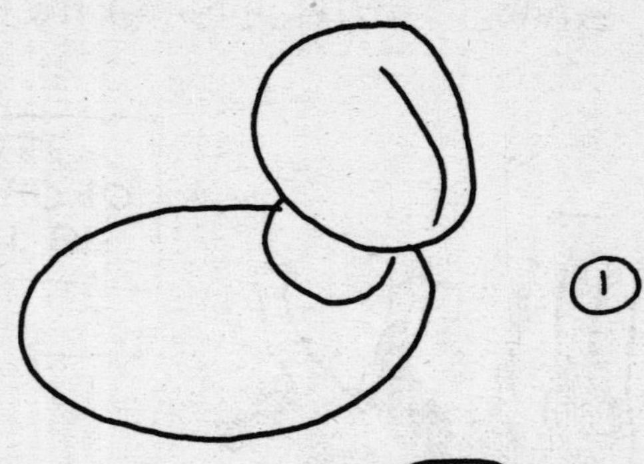

DRAW THE FIRST 2 STEPS LIGHTLY IN PENCIL.

ERASE THE GUIDE LINES AND ADD DETAILS.

DRAW YOUR PICTURE HERE

POODLE

DRAW YOUR PICTURE HERE

FOX TERRIER

DRAW YOUR PICTURE HERE

SCOTTY

①

②

ADD HAIR LINES TO THE BASIC SHAPES.

③

HAIR FOLLOWS THE BASIC SHAPE.

DRAW YOUR PICTURE HERE

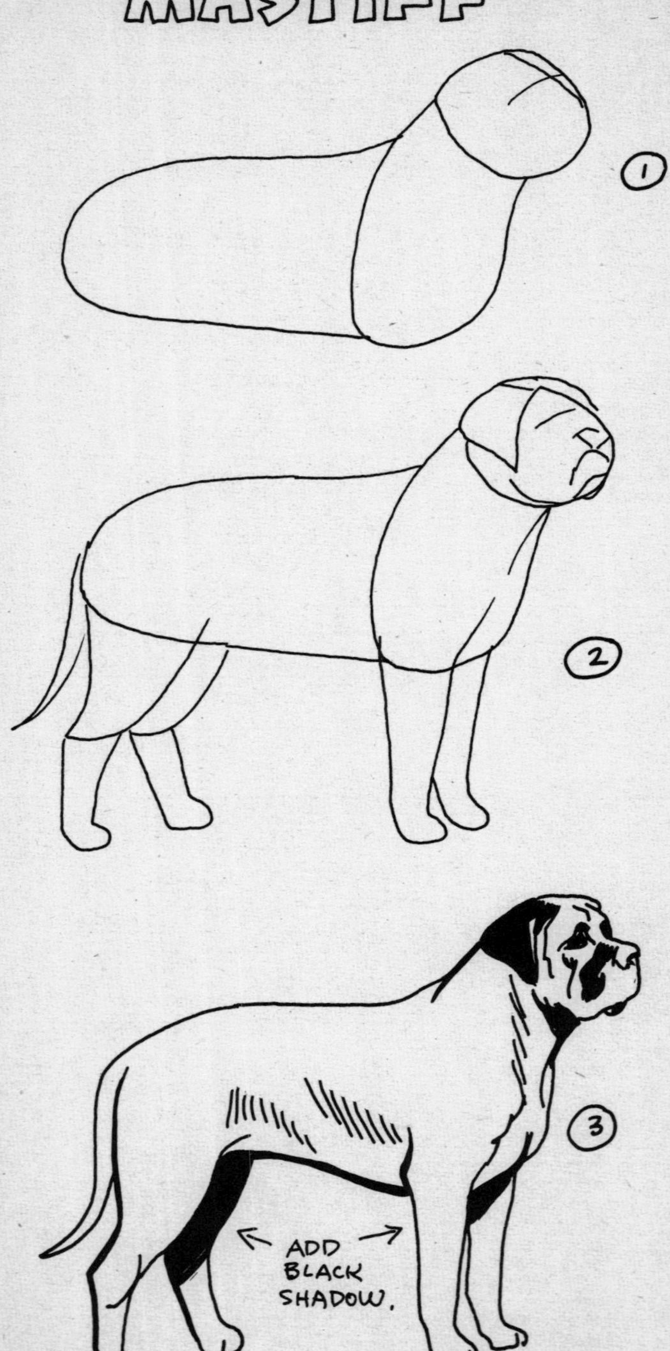
MASTIFF
1
2
3
ADD
BLACK
SHADOW.

DRAW YOUR PICTURE HERE

DACHSHUND

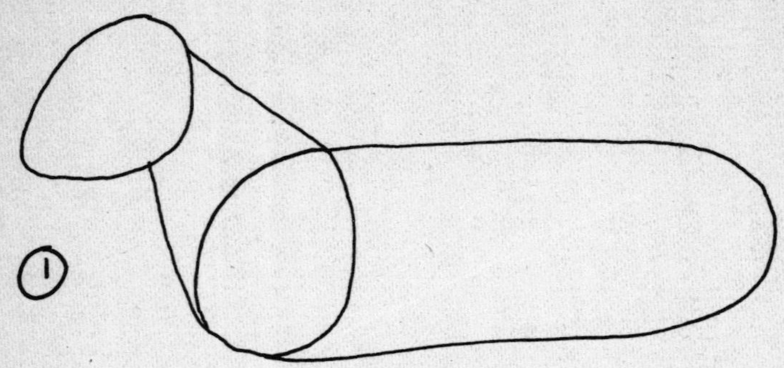

↖ DRAW THIS SHAPE FIRST. THEN ADD THE OTHERS.

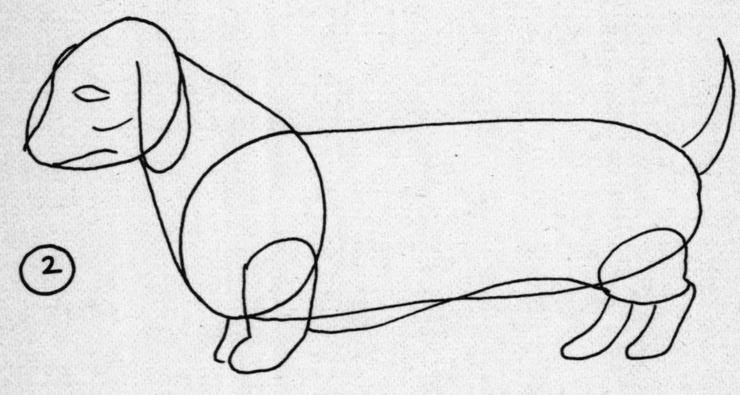

DRAW YOUR PICTURE HERE

FOXHOUND

1
2
3
ADD THE
BLACK DESIGNS
ONLY AFTER
YOU HAVE
COMPLETED
EVERYTHING
ELSE.

DRAW YOUR PICTURE HERE

BULLDOG

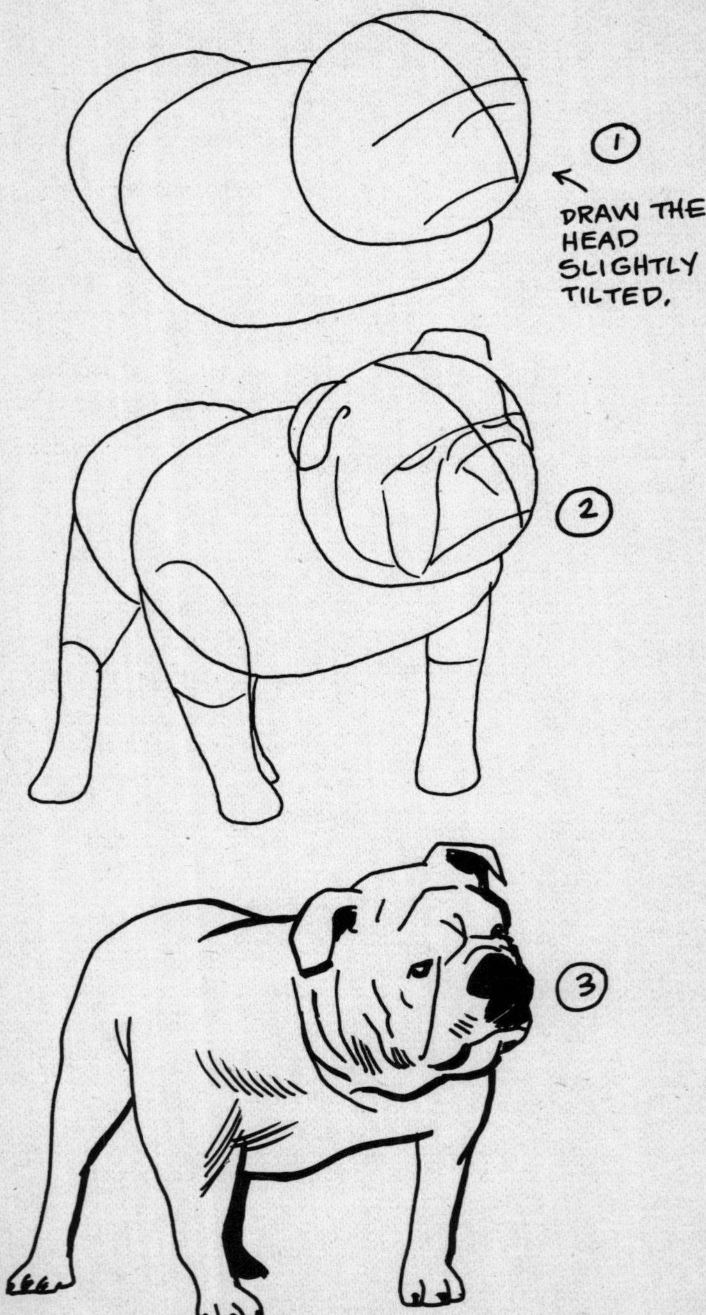

DRAW YOUR PICTURE HERE

AIREDALE

DRAW YOUR PICTURE HERE

BLOODHOUND

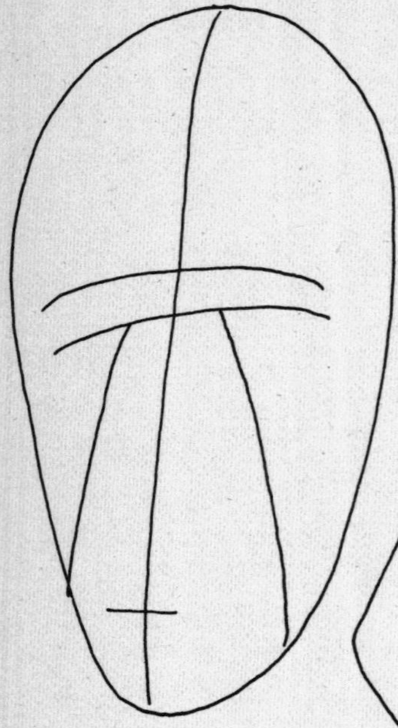

1

2

3

DRAW YOUR PICTURE HERE

COLLIE

DRAW YOUR PICTURE HERE

SHEEP DOG

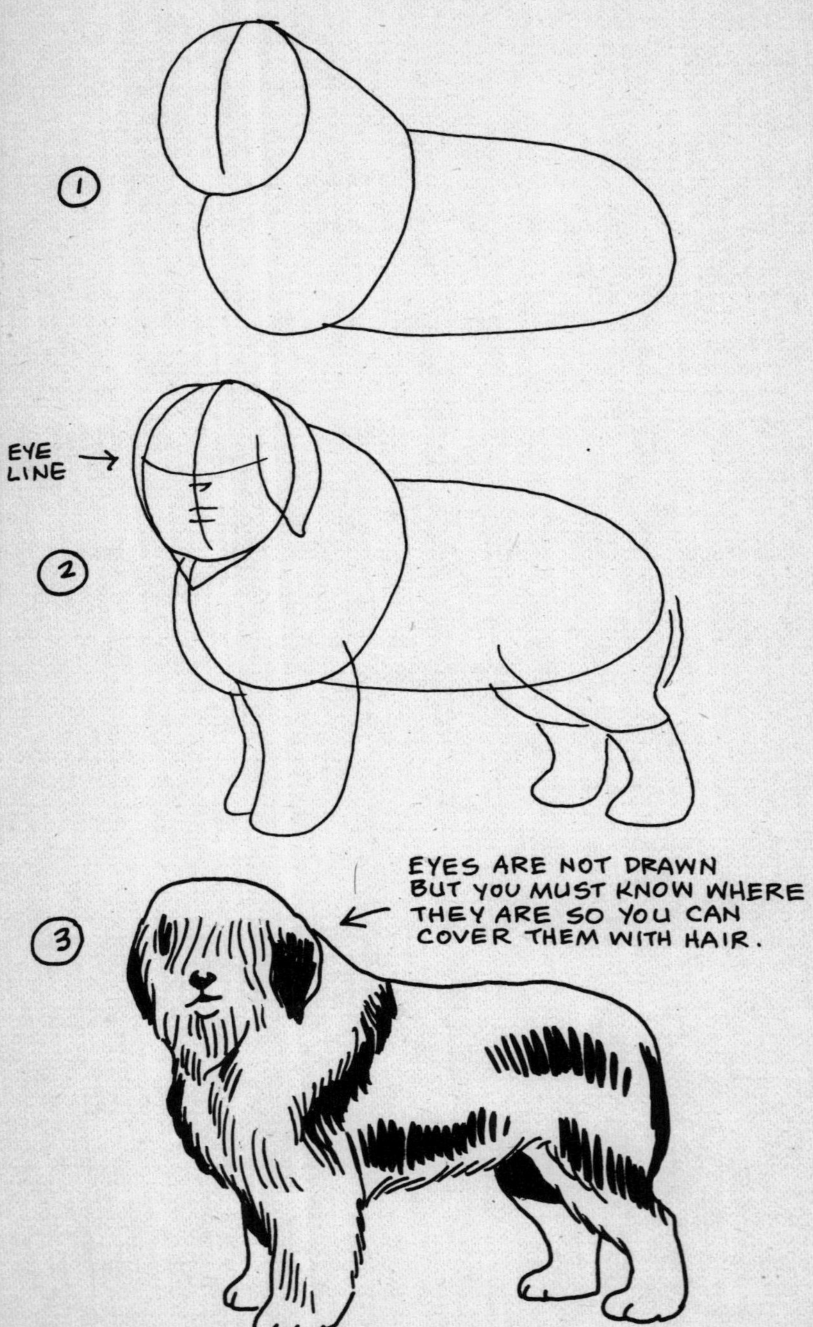
1
EYE LINE
2
EYES ARE NOT DRAWN BUT YOU MUST KNOW WHERE THEY ARE SO YOU CAN COVER THEM WITH HAIR.
3

DRAW YOUR PICTURE HERE

BEAGLE

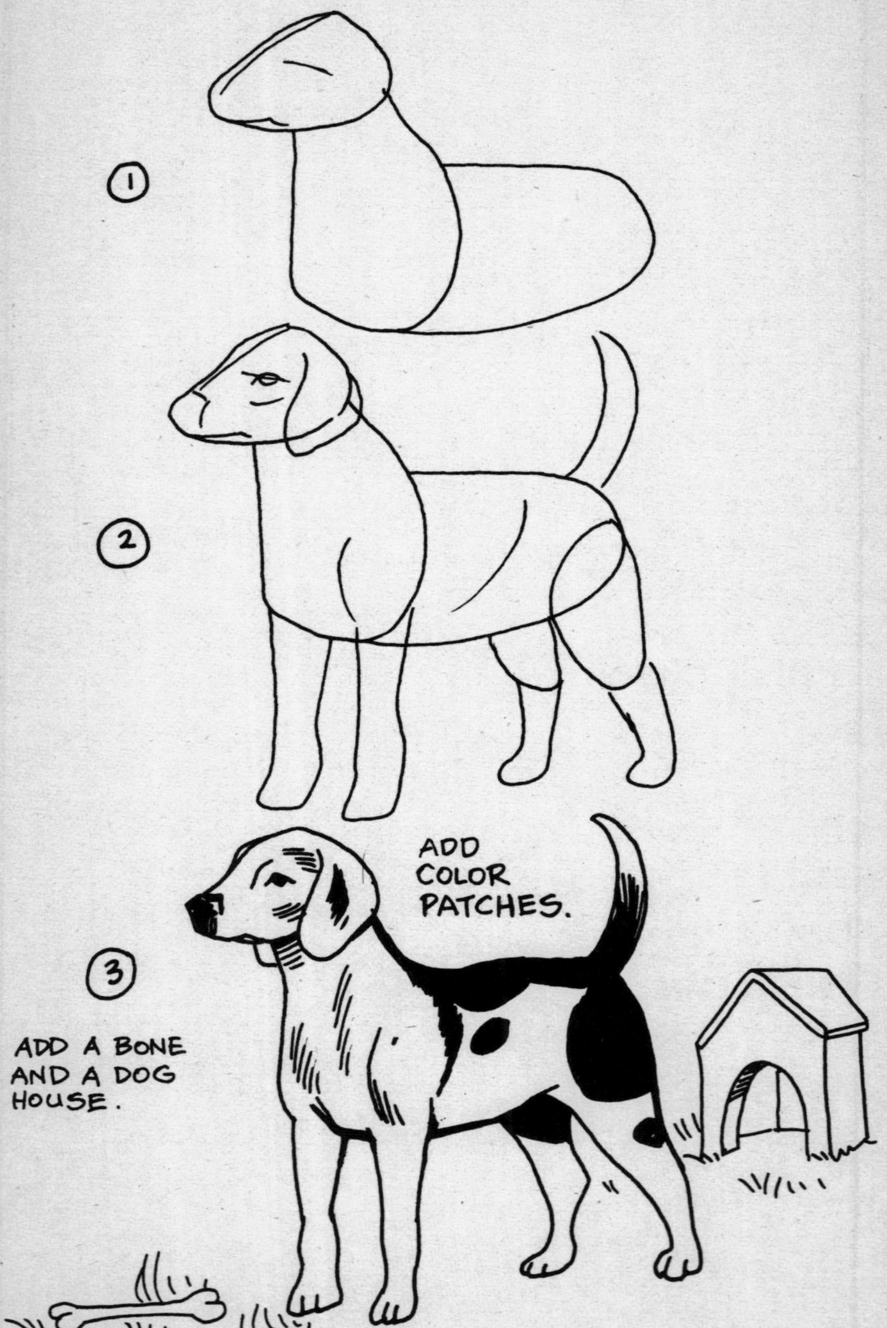

DRAW YOUR PICTURE HERE

DALMATIAN

1
2
3
ADD THE SPOTS
AFTER YOU'VE
COMPLETED THE
REST OF THE
DRAWING.

DRAW YOUR PICTURE HERE

BULL TERRIER

DRAW YOUR PICTURE HERE

KITTEN

DRAW YOUR PICTURE HERE

TABBY

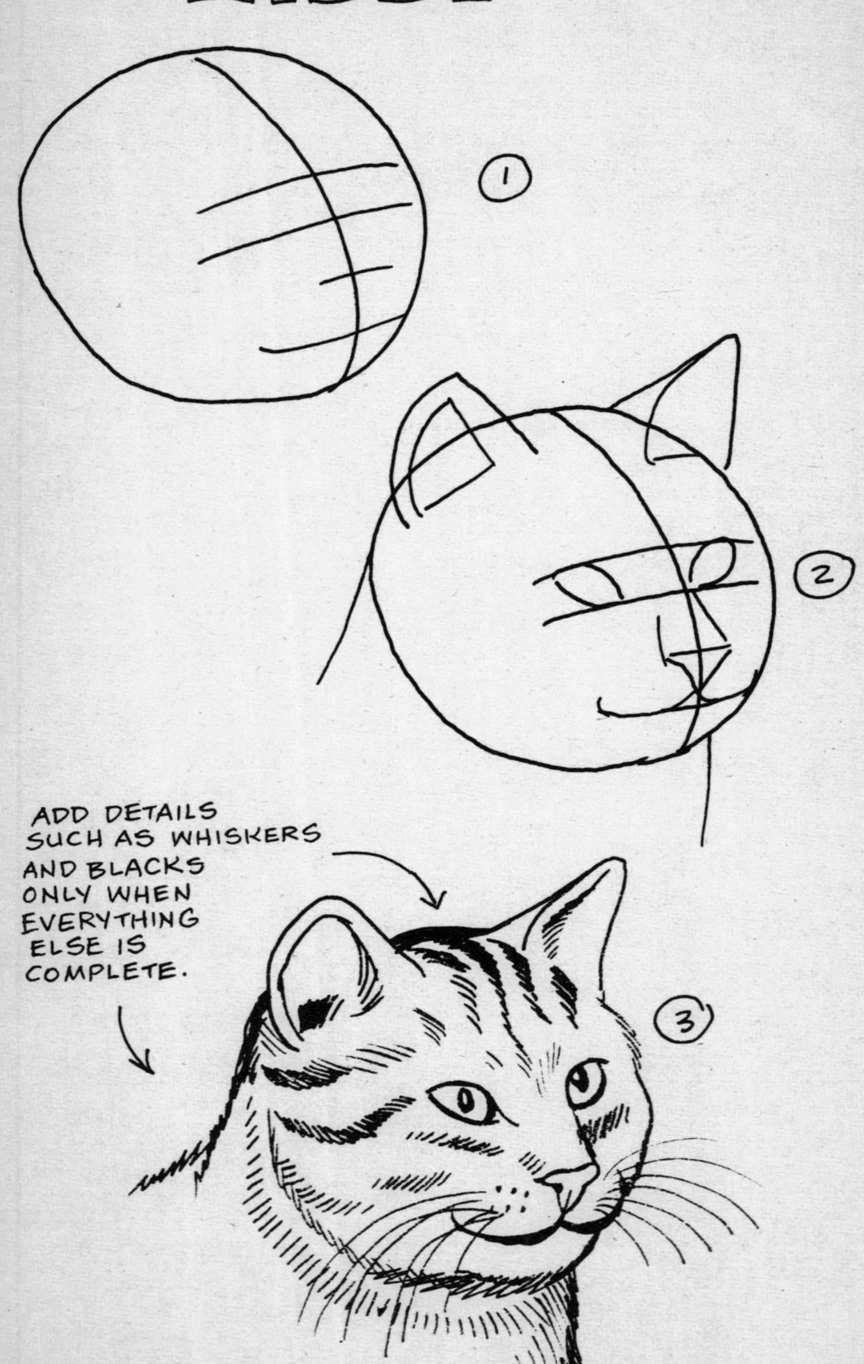
1
2
ADD DETAILS SUCH AS WHISKERS AND BLACKS ONLY WHEN EVERYTHING ELSE IS COMPLETE.
3

DRAW YOUR PICTURE HERE

HUNGRY TABBY

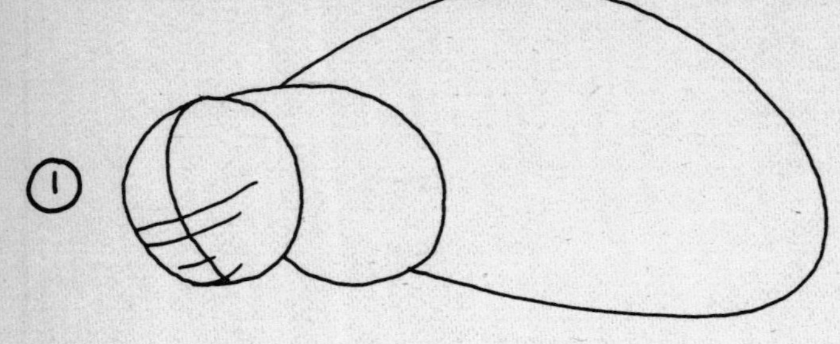

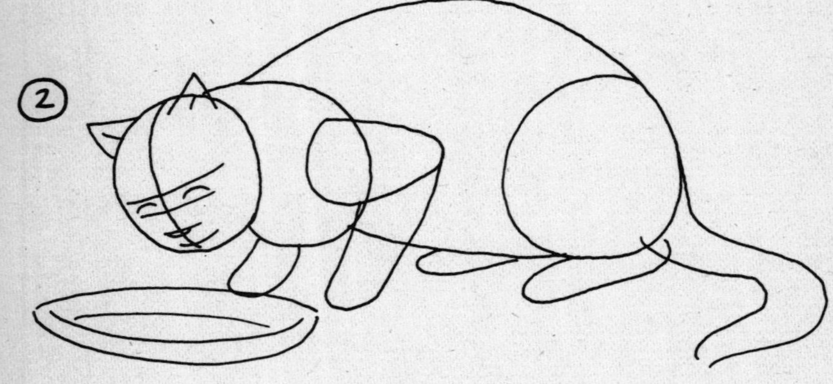

DRAW YOUR PICTURE HERE

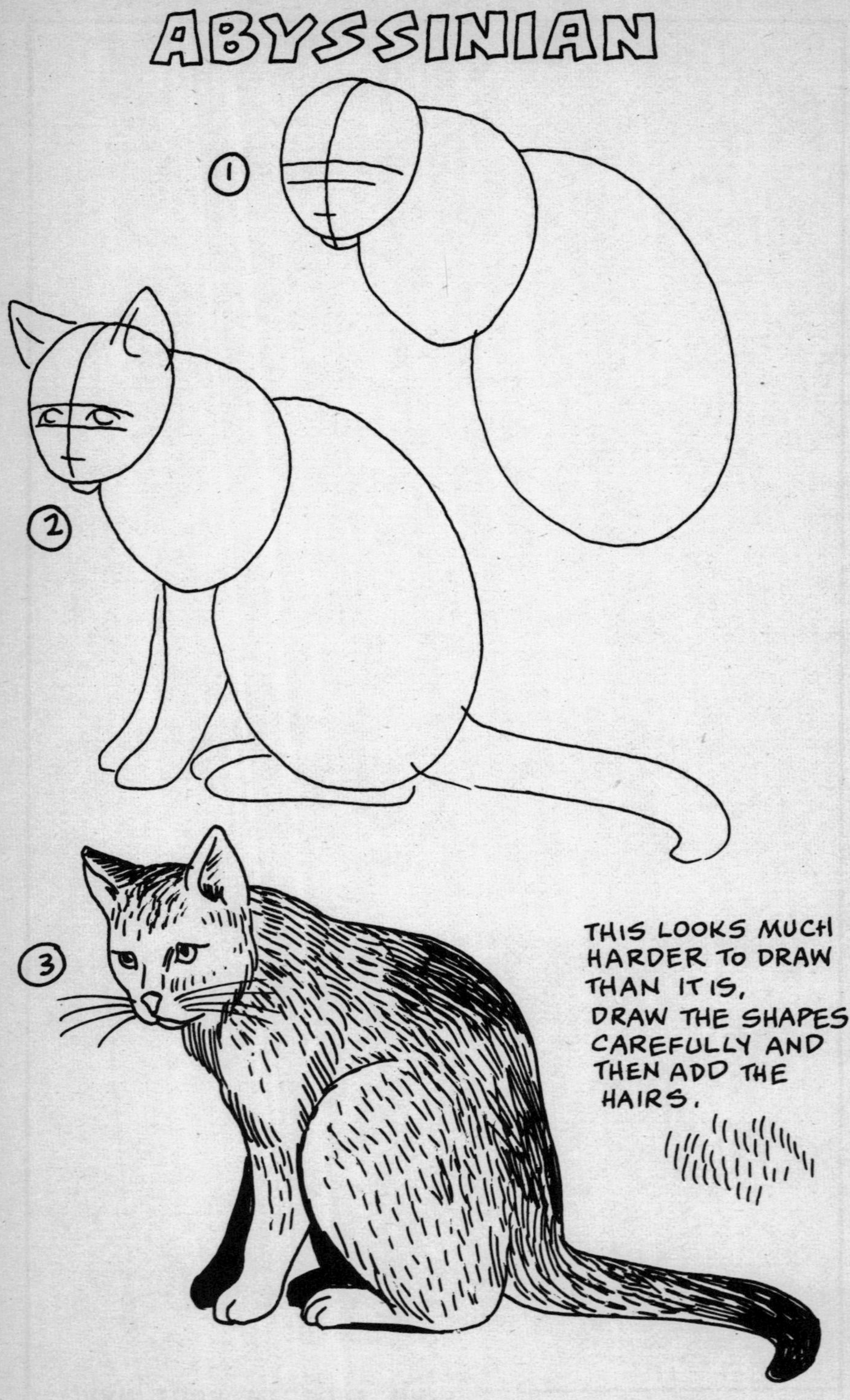
ABYSSINIAN
1
2
3
THIS LOOKS MUCH HARDER TO DRAW THAN IT IS,
DRAW THE SHAPES CAREFULLY AND THEN ADD THE HAIRS.

DRAW YOUR PICTURE HERE

LONGHAIRED

1
2
3
ADD HAIR LINES TO THE WHOLE BODY SHAPES.
NO HAIR LINES ON THE LEG AREAS.

DRAW YOUR PICTURE HERE

SIAMESE

1

2

DRAW THIS SHAPE FIRST – THEN ADD THE OTHERS.

DRAW YOUR PICTURE HERE

DOMESTIC SHORTHAIR

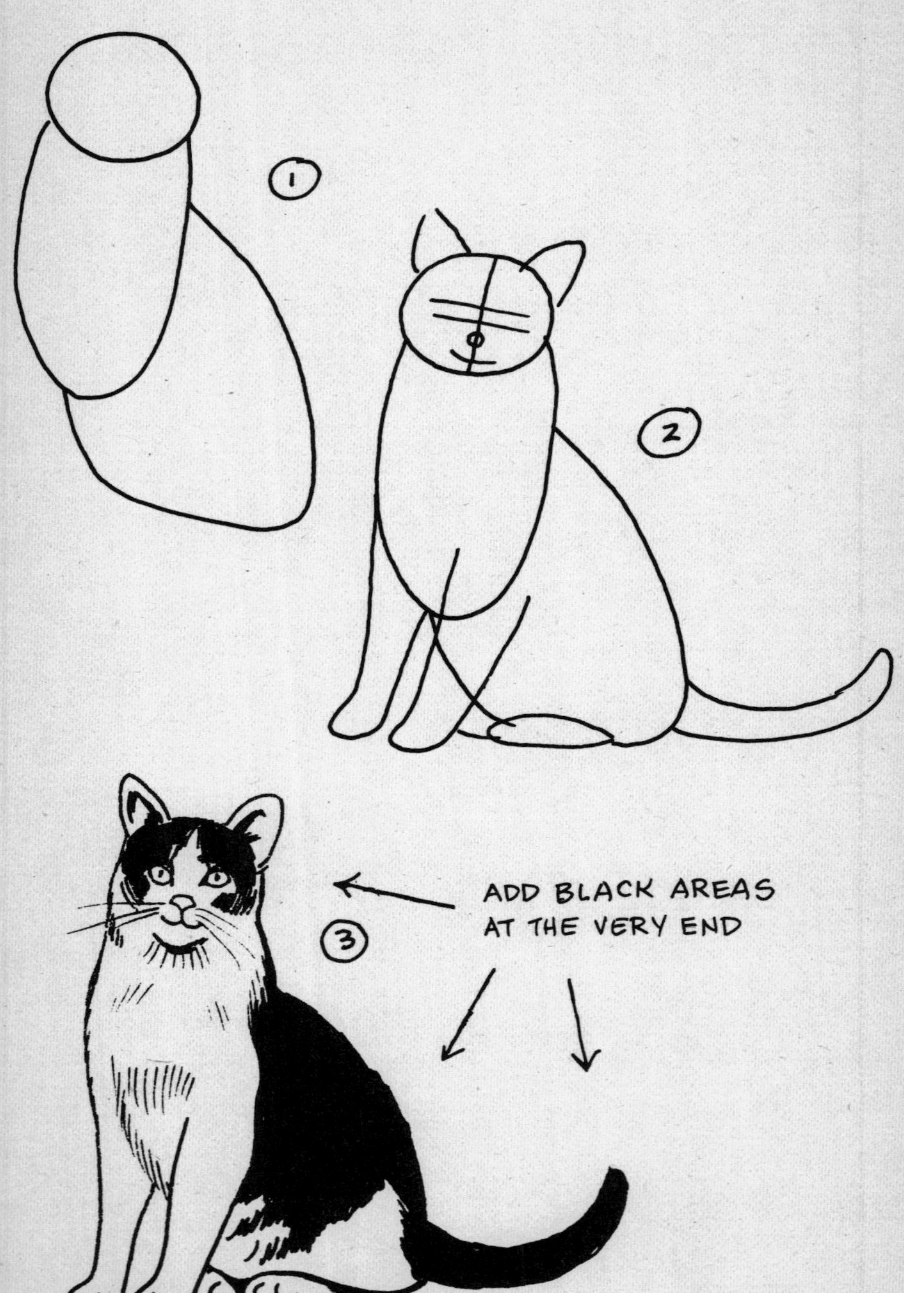

DRAW YOUR PICTURE HERE

DRAW YOUR OWN PICTURE OF A DOG OR CAT HERE –